Look Out!

by Lisa Thompson
illustrated by Lisa Thompson
and
Matthew Stapleton

PICTURE WINDOW BOOKS
Minneapolis, Minnesota

Editor: Jacqueline A. Wolfe
Managing Editor: Catherine Neitge
Story Consultant: Terry Flaherty
Page Production: Melissa Kes/ James Mackey
Creative Director: Keith Griffin
Editorial Director: Carol Jones

First American edition published in 2006 by
Picture Window Books
5115 Excelsior Boulevard
Suite 232
Minneapolis, MN 55416
1-877-845-8392
www.picturewindowbooks.com

First published in Australia in 2004 by
Blake Publishing Pty Ltd
ABN 50 074 266 023
108 Main Rd
Clayton South VIC 3168
© Blake Publishing Pty Ltd Australia 2004

Printed in the United States of America.

Library of Congress Cataloging-in-Publication Data
Thompson, Lisa, 1969-
Look out! / by Lisa Thompson ; illustrated by Lisa Thompson and Matthew Stapleton.— 1st American ed.
p. cm. — (Read-it! chapter books) (Wonder wits)
Summary: Frustrated over their latest invention, the Boomerang ball, Luke and Sophie meet a woman with an interest in accidental inventions who teaches them about serendipity.
ISBN 1-4048-1343-8 (hardcover)
[1. Serendipity—Fiction. 2. Inventions—Fiction.] I. Stapleton, Matthew, ill. II. Title. III. Series.
PZ7.T371634Loo 2005
[Fic]—dc22
2005009828

Table of Contents

More Stuff

"It's no use!" said Luke, kicking a dog bone. "Even food isn't going to get Gizmo to come out. It looks like he's staying where he is."

"Not if I can help it!" said his best friend, Sophie. She peeked into a small tunnel that went under Luke's house.

The Boomerang Ball—

In the past week, Luke's dog, Gizmo, had destroyed seven samples of their latest invention. The Boomerang Ball was meant to come back to you after you had thrown it. Luke and Sophie, however, hadn't been able to perfect the design because Gizmo kept catching the samples and chewing them into pieces.

So Luke put their last ball on a bench where he thought Gizmo couldn't reach it.

But Gizmo got the ball and took it to his favorite hiding spot under the house. He was waiting to be left alone so he could chew it in peace.

"I should never have taken my eyes off that ball, not even for a second," sighed Luke.

"Wait a minute. I've got an idea," said Sophie, jumping to her feet.

Hot tip! Never take

Sophie ran inside the house and grabbed a portable CD player and a CD that belonged to Luke's grandma. She hurried back and crouched outside the opening to the tunnel.

"I don't think Gizmo is going to care if we play him some tunes," said Luke, puzzled.

"He will when he hears what song I'm about to play," she said, loading the CD.

"This CD has the song that the ice cream truck plays when it comes around," Sophie explained.

"You mean the song that makes him bark like crazy and chase the truck?" Luke asked.

Sophie nodded and said, "When I turn this on, Gizmo is going to race out looking for the truck. He will have to drop the ball when he barks."

Ok, what's it going to be?

"Then, one of us will pick up the ball. We'll race out of the yard, leaving Gizmo here. We'll take it to the park and do our test throwing there," said Sophie.

"I hope your plan works," said Luke, staring at Gizmo and the ball under the house. "At least it looks like he hasn't started chewing on it yet."

The ball or the ice cream van?

Sophie switched on the music. For a moment, nothing happened. Then Gizmo raced from under the house. As soon as Gizmo hit daylight, he dropped the ball and began barking like crazy.

Luke swooped. "I've got the ball!" he cried. "Quick! Run for it!"

Sophie sped after Luke. She knew it wouldn't be long before Gizmo realized he'd been tricked. They ran toward the park.

Sorry, Gizmo.

"We did it!" cried Luke, tossing the ball to Sophie.

Sophie inspected the ball and breathed a sigh of relief. It hardly had a mark on it. The park was empty, except for a woman with a picnic basket underneath the giant tree in the far corner.

Sophie was about to throw the ball when she heard loud barking. It came closer.

You've been tricked!

"Oh no, it's Gizmo!" cried Luke. "We forgot to lock the gate!"

Sophie turned to see Gizmo bounding excitedly toward her and the ball.

"Run, Sophie!" yelled Luke. "We'd better split up. Gizmo thinks this is all part of the game."

Sophie ran. Gizmo followed.

"Throw me the ball!" yelled Luke, running toward the giant tree.

Hot tip! #102   Do not look away

Sophie tossed the ball toward Luke without looking. Gizmo changed direction to follow the ball. The ball flew past Luke and disappeared into the giant tree the woman was sitting next to.

"Oh no," Luke groaned.

Gizmo dug his paws into the ground and skidded to a halt. They looked up into the tree.

"You're kidding!" Sophie sighed. "Honestly, what else can happen?"

as you throw the ball!

"I think the ball is lodged in those branches right up near the top, next to that bird's nest," said the woman, pointing as she stood up from her picnic blanket. She wasn't much taller than Luke and Sophie. Her face was round and friendly, and her black, curly hair bounced when she spoke.

A bad situation could be a

"The bottom branches are too high to reach, which means we can't climb the tree. So it's going to be fun to figure out a way to get the ball down. What a wonderful thing to happen!" she said.

"I don't think *wonderful* is the word we'd use," said Luke. "That ball is the last sample of our latest invention."

"And everything has gone wrong while we've been trying to make it," added Sophie.

Gizmo barked and wagged his tail.

"It's not like YOU didn't have anything to do with it, Gizmo!" said Luke.

"I always find that a run of mistakes when I'm inventing leads to all kinds of unexpected opportunities," smiled the woman.

"You're an inventor, too?" asked Sophie.

Mistakes can lead to all kinds

"More like an accidental inventor," she replied. "Inventions that happen by accident are my thing."

The woman sat back on her blanket and said, "Now why don't you both try some of my delicious, edible blunders? They might help us think of a way to get your ball back."

of unexpected opportunities.

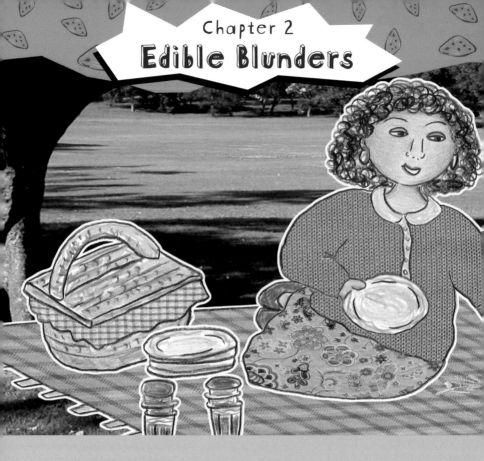

"I guess I should introduce myself," said the woman. "I'm Erica Longly. I take it this beautiful dog is Gizmo?" Gizmo wagged his tail. "And you two are ...?"

"I'm Sophie, and he's Luke," said Sophie, as she and Luke found places on the blanket.

"Well, I'm pleased that chance has let you join me on my picnic," said Erica.

Left turn, right, left again ...

"You see, years ago I came here by mistake and ended up inventing one of my most delicious creations ever." As Erica spoke, she laid out plates for them. "I was catering for a party, and I was running late. I took a wrong turn, then another, and ended up at this park. I was completely lost," she said. "Anyway, I unpacked my basket to get a drink of juice, while I thought about what I was going to do."

"The contents of the basket had fallen everywhere! Sponge cake, nuts, marshmallows, cream, and berries were mixed together. It was a dreadful mess, but it tasted delicious! That's how my award-winning Serendipity Surprise Crumble was invented," Erica said, clapping her hands.

"Serendipity is discovering something good when you're not looking for it. Since then, I've won five food awards for this crumble!"

"Serendipity is discovering something

"So now, when I get a chance, I pack a basket of things that were invented by mistake. I bring them here to celebrate the wonderful accidents and brilliant blunders that occur everywhere. You'd be amazed how many things around us came about accidentally!" Erica exclaimed.

Sophie and Luke were intrigued. They loved finding out how things came to be invented—almost as much as they loved inventing.

good when you're not looking for it."

Erica handed them each a chocolate chip cookie.

"You're not telling me these were an accident!" gasped Luke.

"The story is," said Erica smiling, " in 1930, a woman named Ruth Wakefield ran out of baker's chocolate. She threw in bits of a chocolate bar instead, thinking they'd melt. Only they didn't! When Ruth got the cookies out of the oven, the chocolate bits were still there."

A new taste sensation—

Erica continued, "Ruth had accidentally invented the first batch of delicious chocolate chip cookies!"

"What else is in the basket?" asked Sophie eagerly.

Erica brought out a piece of cheese. "Now, cheese apparently came about after an Arabian traveler poured milk into a carrying pouch made from a lamb's stomach. Later, he opened the pouch and found cheese!"

created totally by accident!

"The pouch still contained the lamb's digestive juices, which helped the hot sun turn the milk into cheese! You know, they still use these digestive juices to make cheese today!" said Erica.

"You mean a lamb's stomach helped invent cheese!" cried Sophie in horror. "Gross!"

"What about Popsicles?" blurted Luke who had spotted them in the basket.

How about that! Unexpected discoveries

"There used to be a drink made with soda water, powder, and water. One evening, a boy left his drink outside, with the stirring stick still in it. It froze overnight. He called them Popsicles," Erica explained. "Now, try some of my Serendipity Surprise." She served up large helpings.

Luke bit into his piece. "It's delicious!" he said, his mouth still full.

Sophie nodded. "It really is an amazing crumble. But ... " she paused, "I'm a bit lost as to what this has to do with getting our ball back."

"You feel lost? Well, that's good!" said Erica, looking more delighted than concerned. "What I mean is, being lost is how I came here and discovered my Serendipity Surprise in the first place."

Feeling lost forces

Erica leaned closer, as though she was about to tell them something very important. "When you feel lost, you come up with new ways of trying to find answers. You see, accidental inventing is all about how you look at things," she said, as she looked inside her basket. "Now what else can I show you?"

you to find new answers.

"An accidental inventor always needs an open mind," Erica explained. "That way, you can turn what seems like a failure to everyone else into a success. Take the Post-it note," she said, pulling out a pack. "No one planned to invent Post-it notes. In fact, the adhesive mix was meant to be sprayed on bulletin boards."

9am Dancing
11am Music
1pm. Singing
3pm Home!

Call
Dentist!

Missing!
One left
Sock
one right
Shoe

39
Clairmont
ave

213

Do
Not
touch!

Dont
forget
to
feed
Dog

"The idea was that people could stick paper to the board, but it didn't catch on. The adhesive sat on the shelf, until one day someone thought the adhesive could be used on the back of page markers—voila! Now Post-it notes are everywhere."

"Lucky they didn't throw the adhesive away," said Sophie, taking the last spoonful of her crumble.

need an open mind.

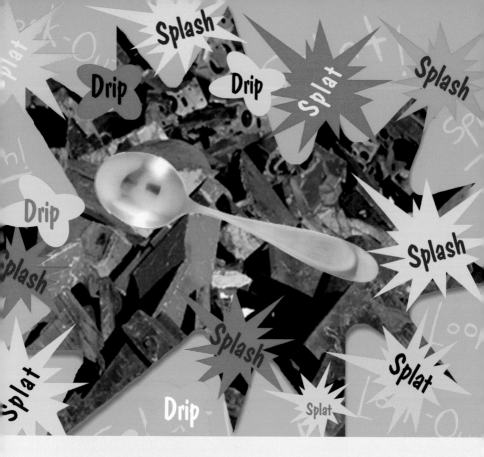

"Actually, throwing things away is how your stainless steel spoon came about," said Erica. "Stainless steel was discovered when someone noticed that a metal sample in a junk pile hadn't rusted."

Suddenly, the birds in the tree above started squawking. They'd discovered there was a ball near their nest. Gizmo leapt off the rug. Food and drinks went everywhere.

Spills are a big part of

"Good one, Giz!" cried Sophie, as she and Luke tried to grab things before they spilt.

"Oh, never mind," said Erica, as she helped them clean up. "Spills are a big part of accidental inventing. Scotchgard, the fabric protector on this blanket, was discovered after a spill. A lab assistant spilled chemicals on his shoes. The researchers noticed that the spot where the chemical had landed remained clean."

accidental inventing.

"Safety glass, dry cleaning, photography, tires, and rayon were all invented because of spills—even the telephone!" said Erica.

"The telephone?" quizzed Luke.

"Sure!" replied Erica. "It was still at an experimental stage when the inventor, Alexander Graham Bell, spilled battery acid near his invention. He called for help, and his words were transmitted by electric currents."

When magical mistakes happen,

"Well, I think Gizmo invented what he usually invents—a mess!" laughed Luke.

"What about inventions that came about when people weren't even thinking about inventing?" asked Sophie.

Erica hunted in her basket again. "Now, I'm sure I packed a few of those. I like to call them my magical mistakes."

Erica held up a matchbox and a melted chocolate bar. "I call these magical mistakes because someone had the magical, inventive eyes to understand what they saw."

"Matches," said Erica, "came about after a chemist stirred a mixture, and a glob formed at the end of the stick. The chemist tried to remove the glob by scraping it against the stone floor. Suddenly, the end of the stick burst into flames, and the match was invented!"

"And the melted chocolate bar?" asked Sophie.

"The chocolate bar isn't the invention," said Erica. "But it revealed the potential of microwave cooking! A scientist was doing an experiment when he realized the experiments had melted the chocolate bar in his pocket. He had stumbled upon microwave cooking accidentally!" Erica exclaimed.

spot magical mistakes.

The top of the tree shook as the birds hopped from branch to branch. The Boomerang Ball began to fall.

"Look out!" yelled Luke.

Gizmo jumped up, caught the ball in his mouth, and ran.

"Oh NO!" cried Luke, chasing after him.

"Well, that solved the problem of getting the ball down," laughed Erica.

A mistake is only a mistake if

"But not getting it back!" said Sophie. "And I don't like our chances of getting it back chew-free." She stood up, ready to join the chase. "Bye, Erica. Thanks for everything."

"Best of luck!" yelled Erica. "Remember, a disaster is often an invention in disguise! As a wise person once said, 'A mistake is only a mistake if you don't learn anything from it!'"

you don't learn anything from it.

Chapter 5

Spotting the Unexpected

By the time Luke and Sophie caught up with Gizmo, the Boomerang Ball was a chewed mess. But this time, they didn't think it was a disaster.

Immediately, Luke and Sophie thought of an invention that was better than the Boomerang Ball. It was something that Gizmo and lots of other dogs like him were barking for.

The Peeler Ball—

A few days later, Sophie had in her hand a ball made up of different layers. "This is what we should have been inventing all along," laughed Sophie.

Luke decided to name it the Peeler Ball. Each layer of the ball could be peeled away or chewed to reveal a different surface. The closer the layers came to the middle of the ball, the harder they were to chew.

layers of doggie fun.

Every layer of the ball had a different texture. It could be spiked, grooved, bumpy, or smooth.

Sophie threw the ball to Luke.

"Gizmo will be so excited when he sees this," he said with a grin.

"It will make up for the trick we played with the music," said Sophie. "I think it's time we let him in."

Spiked, grooved, bumpy,

Luke opened the door, and Gizmo bounded excitedly into the work shed. Luke tossed him the ball. "There you go, Giz. It's the ball you've been trying to tell us to invent."

Gizmo chewed and pawed the ball. Then, he grabbed it in his mouth and tossed it high. The ball landed on one of the workbenches. In an instant, Gizmo leapt after it.

smooth, shiny, rough ...

"Giz, NO!" cried Luke, but it was too late. Sophie and Luke ducked for cover. Boxes, jars, and half-finished inventions crashed, spilled, and toppled everywhere.

"I wonder what Gizmo's invented this time?" giggled Sophie.

Always remember—a disaster

"I'm not sure," sighed Luke, surveying the disaster zone Gizmo had just created.

"Whatever it is, it's one accidental invention that is very well-disguised! But," Sophie said smiling, "I'm doing my best to keep an open mind!"

could just be an invention in disguise.

Look Out

Check out the accidents, mistakes, and blunders that led to these inventions!

Band-Aids

In a moment of inspiration, an employee of the Johnson & Johnson company, Earl Dickson, came up with a product almost everyone will use once in their lives. When tending to a small cut on his wife, Earl realized the cut was too small for a bandage. Instead, he cut a little piece of gauze and placed it at the center of an adhesive strip to cover the wound. Earl had just invented the Band-Aid!

Tea Bags

Thomas Sullivan was a tea and coffee merchant who often sent his customers samples in cans. In 1904, Sullivan decided it would be simpler and cheaper to send his tea samples in hand-sewn silk bags. They became a hit, and tea bags spread all over the world.

The Flashlight

The flashlight began as a novelty item called the Electric Flowerpot. It's not surprising that few people were interested in such a strange product. It was only after the pot was discarded and the product was renamed the Portable Electric Light that it became the handy item it is today!

Worcestershire Sauce

When two chemists from Worcester, England, John Lea and William Perrins, first made a sauce recipe that a customer had given them, they thought it tasted terrible! They took the batch of jars they had poured the sauce into down to their cellar and forgot about them. Some time later, the jars were coated in dust and about to be thrown out. The two chemists tasted the sauce once again. To their surprise, it tasted fantastic! Their once terrible tasting sauce had aged and matured. Instead of ending up in the garbage, the sauce became known as Worcestershire Sauce, and is now eaten all over the world!

45

Cellophane

Charles Brandenberger was a Swiss chemist who tried to invent a stain-proof tablecloth. He failed. Instead, he came up with a flimsy material he called cellophane. It became one of the world's most popular and useful food wraps!

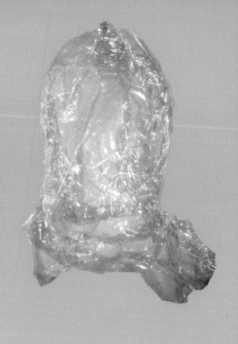

Chewing Gum

Charles Adams was trying to get the dried sap of the sapodilla tree (a substance known as chicle) to be a substitute for rubber, but all his experiments failed. Sitting in his workshop one day, tired and discouraged, he popped some chicle in his mouth and began to chew it, just as the Mayans of Mexico had been doing for centuries. Suddenly, he hit upon the idea of adding flavoring to chicle. Shortly after, Charles Adams opened the world's first chewing gum factory and made a fortune.

Potato Chips

In 1853, a chef by the name of George Crum decided to play a trick on a very fussy guest who kept complaining about his potatoes. Crum produced a bowl of potatoes that were cut very thin and very crisp. The guest loved them and raved about them! George Crum's unusual style of potato chips became a restaurant favorite. Now, more than one hundred and fifty years later, the chip that came about because of a practical joke is available in hundreds of varieties and eaten all over the world!

Bricks

Some archaeologists believe that the first bricks may have been made accidentally. The theory is that mud and silt from the Nile River would have hardened along the banks into slabs. An Egyptian walking along the Nile may have seen the slabs and realized that they could be shaped into blocks for buildings.

SO LOOK OUT! The next mistake YOU make may be a great invention!

Read all about Luke and Sophie's unusual adventures in these great books!

1. Artrageous
2. Wonder Worlds
3. Wild Ideas
4. Look Out!
5. What's Next?
6. Game Plan
7. Gadget Hero
8. Bony Puzzle

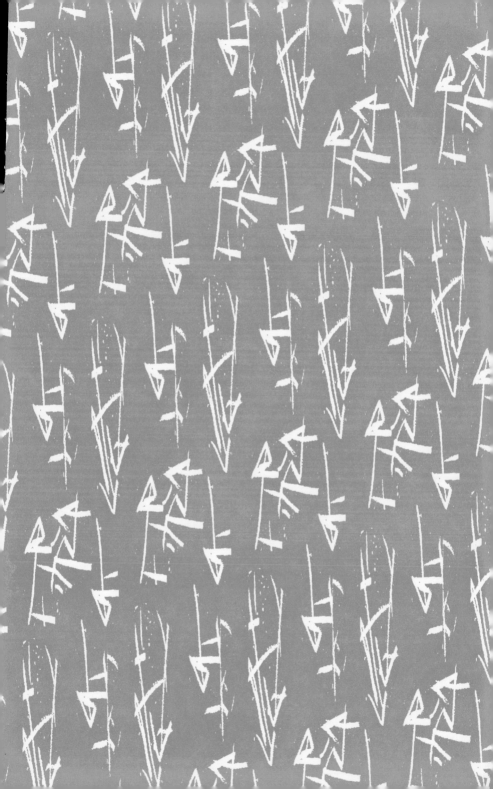

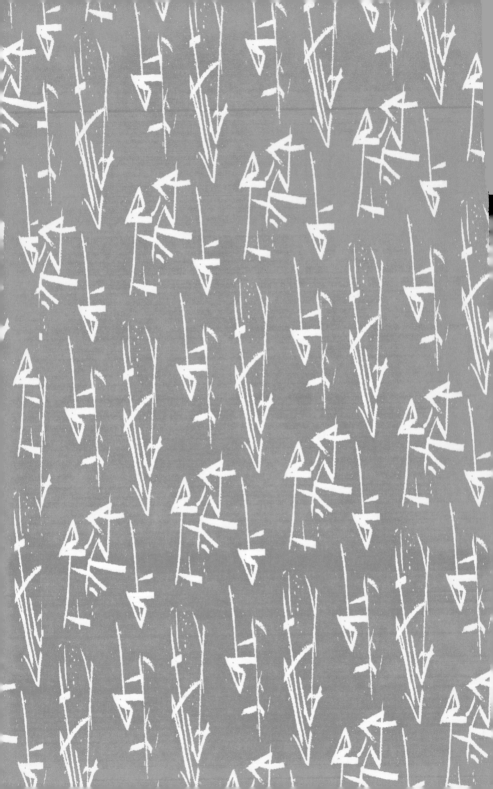